'It was as if the sea, breaking down the wall protecting all the homes of the town, had sent a wave over her head' . . .

JOSEPH CONRAD
Born 1857, Berdychiv, Russia
Died 1924, Bishopsbourne, England

'To-morrow' was first published in 1902.

CONRAD IN PENGUIN CLASSICS
Heart of Darkness
Lord Jim
Nostromo
The Secret Agent
The Secret Sharer and Other Stories
Typhoon and Other Stories
Under Western Eyes

This book is to be returned on or **before**
the last date stamped below. Ten 10/18

PENGUIN BOOKS

PENGUIN CLASSICS

Published by the Penguin Group
Penguin Books Ltd, 80 Strand, London WC2R ORL, England
Penguin Group (USA) Inc., 375 Hudson Street, New York, New York 10014, USA
Penguin Group (Canada), 90 Eglinton Avenue East, Suite 700, Toronto, Ontario,
Canada M4P 2Y3 (a division of Pearson Penguin Canada Inc.)
Penguin Ireland, 25 St Stephen's Green, Dublin 2, Ireland
(a division of Penguin Books Ltd)
Penguin Group (Australia), 707 Collins Street, Melbourne, Victoria 3008, Australia
(a division of Pearson Australia Group Pty Ltd)
Penguin Books India Pvt Ltd, 11 Community Centre, Panchsheel Park,
New Delhi – 110 017, India
Penguin Group (NZ), 67 Apollo Drive, Rosedale, Auckland 0632, New Zealand
(a division of Pearson New Zealand Ltd)
Penguin Books (South Africa) (Pty) Ltd, Block D, Rosebank Office Park,
181 Jan Smuts Avenue, Parktown North, Gauteng 2193, South Africa

Penguin Books Ltd, Registered Offices: 80 Strand, London WC2R ORL, England

www.penguin.com

This edition published in Penguin Classics 2015
001

Set in 10/14.5 pt Baskerville 10 Pro
Typeset by Jouve (UK), Milton Keynes
Printed in Great Britain by Clays Ltd, St Ives plc

A CIP catalogue record for this book is available from the British Library

ISBN: 978-0-141-39849-5

www.greenpenguin.co.uk

MIX
Paper from
responsible sources
FSC® C018179
www.fsc.org

Penguin Books is committed to a sustainable
future for our business, our readers and our planet.
This book is made from Forest Stewardship
Council™ certified paper.

To-morrow

What was known of Captain Hagberd in the little seaport of Colebrook was not exactly in his favour. He did not belong to the place. He had come to settle there under circumstances not at all mysterious – he used to be very communicative about them at the time – but extremely morbid and unreasonable. He was possessed of some little money evidently, because he bought a plot of ground, and had a pair of ugly yellow brick cottages run up very cheaply. He occupied one of them himself and let the other to Josiah Carvil – blind Carvil, the retired boat-builder – a man of evil repute as a domestic tyrant.

These cottages had one wall in common, shared in a line of iron railing dividing their front gardens; a wooden fence separated their back gardens. Miss Bessie Carvil was allowed, as it were of right, to throw over it the tea-cloths, blue rags, or an apron that wanted drying.

'It rots the wood, Bessie my girl,' the captain would remark mildly, from his side of the fence, each time he saw her exercising that privilege.

She was a tall girl; the fence was low, and she could spread her elbows on the top. Her hands would be red with the bit of washing she had done, but her forearms were white and shapely, and she would look at her father's landlord in silence – in an informed silence which had an air of knowledge, expectation, and desire.

'It rots the wood,' repeated Captain Hagberd. 'It is the only unthrifty, careless habit I know in you. Why don't you have a clothes-line out in your back yard?'

Miss Carvil would say nothing to this – she only shook her head negatively. The tiny back yard on her side had a few stone-bordered little beds of black earth, in which the simple flowers she found time to cultivate appeared somehow extravagantly over-grown, as if belonging to an exotic clime; and Captain Hagberd's upright, hale person, clad in No. 1 sail-cloth from head to foot, would be emerging knee-deep out of rank grass and the tall weeds on his side of the fence. He appeared, with the colour and uncouth stiffness of the extraordinary material in which he chose to clothe himself – 'for the time being,' would be his mumbled remark to any observation on the subject – like a man roughened out of granite, stand-ing in a wilderness not big enough for a decent billiard-room. A heavy figure of a man of stone, with a red handsome face, a blue wandering eye, and a great white beard flowing to his waist and never trimmed as far as Colebrook knew.

Seven years before, he had seriously answered, 'Next month, I think,' to the chaffing attempt to secure his custom made by that distinguished local wit, the Colebrook barber, who happened to be sit-ting insolently in the tap-room of the New Inn near the harbour, where the captain had entered to buy an ounce of tobacco. After paying for his purchase with three half-pence extracted from the corner of a handkerchief which he carried in the cuff of his sleeve, Captain Hagberd went out. As soon as the door was shut the barber laughed. 'The old one and the young one will be strolling arm in arm to get shaved in my place presently. The tailor shall be set to work, and the barber, and the candlestick maker; high old times are coming for Colebrook; they are coming, to be sure. It used to be "next week," now it has come to "next month," and so on – soon it will be next spring, for all I know.'

Noticing a stranger listening to him with a vacant grin, he explained, stretching out his legs cynically, that this queer old Hagberd, a retired coasting-skipper, was waiting for the return of a son of his. The boy had been driven away from home, he shouldn't wonder; had run away to sea and had never been heard of since. Put to rest in Davy Jones's locker this many a day, as likely as not. That old man came flying to Colebrook three years ago all in black broadcloth (had lost his wife lately then), getting out of a third-class smoker as if the devil had been at his heels; and the only thing that brought him down was a letter – a hoax probably. Some joker had written to him about a seafaring man with some such name who was supposed to be hanging about some girl or other, either in Colebrook or in the neighbourhood. 'Funny, ain't it?' The old chap had been advertising in the London papers for Harry Hagberd, and offering rewards for any sort of likely information. And the barber would go on to describe, with sardonic gusto, how that stranger in mourning had been seen exploring the country, in carts, on foot, taking everybody into his confidence, visiting all the inns and alehouses for miles around, stopping people on the road with his questions, looking into the very ditches almost; first in the greatest excitement, then with a plodding sort of perseverance, growing slower and slower; and he could not even tell you plainly how his son looked. The sailor was supposed to be one of two that had left a timber ship, and to have been seen dangling after some girl; but the old man described a boy of fourteen or so – 'a clever-looking, high-spirited boy.' And when people only smiled at this he would rub his forehead in a confused sort of way before he slunk off, looking offended. He found nobody, of course; not a trace of anybody – never heard of anything worth belief, at any rate; but he had not been able somehow to tear himself away from Colebrook.

'It was the shock of this disappointment, perhaps, coming soon after the loss of his wife, that had driven him crazy on that point,' the barber suggested, with an air of great psychological insight. After a time the old man abandoned the active search. His son had evidently gone away; but he settled himself to wait. His son had been once at least in Colebrook in preference to his native place. There must have been some reason for it, he seemed to think, some very powerful inducement, that would bring him back to Colebrook again.

'Ha, ha, ha! Why, of course, Colebrook. Where else? That's the only place in the United Kingdom for your long-lost sons. So he sold up his old home in Colchester, and down he comes here. Well, it's a craze, like any other. Wouldn't catch me going crazy over any of my youngsters clearing out. I've got eight of them at home.' The barber was showing off his strength of mind in the midst of a laughter that shook the tap-room.

Strange, though, that sort of thing, he would confess, with the frankness of a superior intelligence, seemed to be catching. His establishment, for instance, was near the harbour, and whenever a sailorman came in for a hair-cut or a shave – if it was a strange face he couldn't help thinking directly, 'Suppose he's the son of old Hagberd!' He laughed at himself for it. It was a strong craze. He could remember the time when the whole town was full of it. But he had his hopes of the old chap yet. He would cure him by a course of judicious chaffing. He was watching the progress of the treatment. Next week – next month – next year! When the old skipper had put off the date of that return till next year, he would be well on his way to not saying any more about it. In other matters he was quite rational, so this, too, was bound to come. Such was the barber's firm opinion.

Nobody had ever contradicted him; his own hair had gone grey since that time, and Captain Hagberd's beard had turned quite white, and had acquired a majestic flow over the No. 1 canvas suit, which he had made for himself secretly with tarred twine, and had assumed suddenly, coming out in it one fine morning, whereas the evening before he had been seen going home in his mourning of broadcloth. It caused a sensation in the High Street – shopkeepers coming to their doors, people in the houses snatching up their hats to run out – a stir at which he seemed strangely surprised at first, and then scared; but his only answer to the wondering questions was that startled and evasive, 'For the present.'

That sensation had been forgotten long ago; and

Captain Hagberd himself, if not forgotten, had come to be disregarded – the penalty of dailiness – as the sun itself is disregarded unless it makes its power felt heavily. Captain Hagberd's movements showed no infirmity: he walked stiffly in his suit of canvas, a quaint and remarkable figure; only his eyes wandered more furtively perhaps than of yore. His manner abroad had lost its excitable watchfulness; it had become puzzled and diffident, as though he had suspected that there was somewhere about him something slightly compromising, some embarrassing oddity; and yet had remained unable to discover what on earth this something wrong could be.

He was unwilling now to talk with the townsfolk. He had earned for himself the reputation of an awful skinflint, of a miser, in the matter of living. He mumbled regretfully in the shops, bought inferior scraps of meat after long hesitations; and discouraged all allusions to his costume. It was as the barber had foretold. For all one could tell, he had recovered already from the disease of hope; and only Miss Bessie Carvil knew that he said nothing about his son's return because with him it was no longer 'next week,' 'next month,' or even 'next year.' It was 'to-morrow.'

In their intimacy of back yard and front garden he talked with her paternally, reasonably, and dogmatically, with a touch of arbitrariness. They met on the ground of unreserved confidence, which was authenticated by an affectionate wink now and then. Miss Carvil had come to look forward rather to these winks. At first they had discomposed her: the poor fellow was mad. Afterwards she had learned to laugh at them: there was no harm in him. Now she was aware of an unacknowledged, pleasurable, incredulous emotion, expressed by a faint blush. He winked not in the least vulgarly; his thin red face, with a well-modelled curved nose, had a sort of distinction – the more so that when he talked to her he looked with a steadier and more intelligent glance. A handsome, hale, upright, capable man, with a white beard. You did not think of his age. His son, he affirmed, had resembled him amazingly from his earliest babyhood.

Harry would be one-and-thirty next July, he declared. Proper age to get married with a nice, sensible girl that could appreciate a good home. He was

9

a very high-spirited boy. High-spirited husbands were the easiest to manage. These mean, soft chaps, that you would think butter wouldn't melt in their mouths, were the ones to make a woman thoroughly miserable. And there was nothing like home – a fireside – a good roof: no turning out of your warm bed in all sorts of weather. 'Eh, my dear?'

Captain Hagberd had been one of those sailors that pursue their calling within sight of land. One of the many children of a bankrupt farmer, he had been apprenticed hurriedly to a coasting-skipper, and had remained on the coast all his sea life. It must have been a hard one at first: he had never taken to it; his affection turned to the land, with its innumerable houses, with its quiet lives gathered round its firesides. Many sailors feel and profess a rational dislike for the sea, but his was a profound and emotional animosity, as if the love of the stabler element had been bred into him through many generations.

'People did not know what they let their boys in for when they let them go to sea,' he expounded to Bessie. 'As soon make convicts of them at once.' He did not believe you ever got used to it. The weariness of such a life got worse as you got older. What sort of trade was it in which more than half your time you did not put your foot inside your house? Directly you got out to sea you had no means of knowing what went on at home. One might have thought him weary of distant voyages; and the longest he had ever made had lasted a fortnight, of which the most part had been spent at anchor, sheltering from the weather. As soon as his wife had inherited a house and enough to live on (from a bachelor uncle who had made some money in the coal business) he threw up his command of an East-coast collier with a feeling as though he had escaped from the galleys. After all these years he might have counted on the fingers of his two hands all the days he had been out of sight of England. He had never known what it was to be out of soundings. 'I have never been further than eighty fathoms from the land' was one of his boasts.

Bessie Carvil heard all these things. In front of their cottage grew an under-sized ash; and on summer afternoons she would bring out a chair on the grass-plot and sit down with her sewing. Captain Hagberd, in his canvas suit, leaned on a spade. He dug every day in his front plot. He turned it over and over several times every year, but was not going to plant anything 'just at present.'

To Bessie Carvil he would state more explicitly: 'Not till our Harry comes home to-morrow.' And she had heard this formula of hope so often that it only awakened the vaguest pity in her heart for that hopeful old man.

Everything was put off in that way, and everything was being prepared likewise for to-morrow. There was a boxful of packets of various flower-seeds to choose from, for the front garden. 'He will doubtless let you have your say about that, my dear,' Captain Hagberd intimated to her across the railing.

Miss Bessie's head remained bowed over her work. She had heard all this so many times. But now and then she would rise, lay down her sewing, and come slowly to the fence. There was a charm in these gentle ravings. He was determined that his son should not go away again for the want of a home all ready for him. He had been filling the other cottage with all sorts of furniture. She imagined it all new, fresh with varnish, piled up as in a warehouse. There would be tables wrapped up in sacking; rolls of carpets thick and vertical like fragments of columns; the gleam of white marble tops in the dimness of the drawn blinds. Captain Hagberd always described his purchases to her carefully, as to a person having a legitimate interest in them. The overgrown yard of his cottage could be laid over with concrete . . . after to-morrow.

'We may just as well do away with the fence. You could have your drying-line out, quite clear of your flowers.' He winked, and she would blush faintly.

This madness that had entered her life through the kind impulses of her heart had reasonable details. What if some day his son returned? But she could not even be quite sure that he ever had a son; and if he existed anywhere, he had been too long away. When Captain Hagberd got excited in his talk she would steady him by a pretence of belief, laughing a little to salve her conscience.

Only once she had tried pityingly to throw some doubt on that hope doomed to disappointment, but the effect of her attempt had scared her very much. All at once over that man's face there came an expression of horror and incredulity, as though he had seen a crack open out in the firmament.

'You – you – you don't think he's drowned!'

For a moment he seemed to her ready to go out of his mind, for in his ordinary state she thought him more sane than people gave him credit for. On that occasion the violence of the emotion was followed by a most paternal and complacent recovery.

'Don't alarm yourself, my dear,' he said a little cunningly. 'The sea can't keep him. He does not belong to it. None of us Hagberds ever did belong to it. Look at me; I didn't get drowned. Moreover, he isn't a sailor at all; and if he is not a sailor, he's bound to come back. There's nothing to prevent him coming back . . .'

His eyes began to wander.

'To-morrow.'

She never tried again, for fear the man should go out of his mind on the spot. He depended on her. She seemed the only sensible person in the town; and he would congratulate himself frankly before her face on having secured such a level-headed wife for his son. The rest of the town, he confided to her once, in a fit of temper, was certainly queer. The way they looked at you – the way they talked to you! He had never got on with any one in the place. Didn't like the people. He would not have left his own country if it had not been clear that his son had taken a fancy to Colebrook.

She humoured him in silence, listening patiently by the fence; crocheting with downcast eyes. Blushes came with difficulty on her dead-white complexion, under the negligently twisted opulence of mahogany-coloured hair. Her father was frankly carroty.

She had a full figure; a tired, unrefreshed face. When Captain Hagberd vaunted the necessity and propriety of a home and the delights of one's own fireside, she smiled a little, with her lips only. Her home delights had been confined to the nursing of her father during the ten best years of her life.

A bestial roaring coming out of an upstairs window would interrupt their talk. She would begin at once to roll up her crochet-work or fold her sewing, without the slightest sign of haste. Meanwhile the howls and roars of her name would go on, making the fishermen strolling upon the sea-wall on the other side of the road turn their heads towards the cottages. She would go in slowly at the front door, and a moment afterwards there would fall a profound silence. Presently she would reappear, leading by the hand a man, gross and unwieldy like a hippopotamus, with a bad-tempered, surly face.

He was a widowed boat-builder, whom blindness had overtaken years before in the full flush of business. He behaved to his daughter as if she had been responsible for its incurable character. He had been heard to bellow at the top of his voice, as if to defy Heaven, that he did not care: he had made enough money to have ham and eggs for his breakfast every morning. He thanked God for it, in a fiendish tone as though he were cursing.

Captain Hagberd had been so unfavourably impressed by his tenant that once he told Miss Bessie, 'He is a very extravagant fellow, my dear.'

She was knitting that day, finishing a pair of socks for her father, who expected her to keep up the supply dutifully. She hated knitting, and, as she was just at the heel part, she had to keep her eyes on her needles.

'Of course it isn't as if he had a son to provide for,' Captain Hagberd went on a little vacantly. 'Girls, of course, don't require so much – h'm – h'm. They don't run away from home, my dear.'

'No,' said Miss Bessie, quietly.

Captain Hagberd, amongst the mounds of turned-up earth, chuckled. With his maritime rig, his weather-beaten face, his beard of Father Neptune, he resembled a deposed sea-god who had exchanged the trident for the spade.

'And he must look upon you as already provided for, in a manner. That's the best of it with the girls. The husbands . . .' He winked. Miss Bessie, absorbed in her knitting, coloured faintly.

'Bessie! my hat!' old Carvil bellowed out suddenly. He had been sitting under the tree mute and motionless, like an idol of some remarkably monstrous superstition. He never opened his mouth but to howl for her, at her, sometimes about her; and then he did not moderate the terms of his abuse. Her system was never to answer him at all; and he kept up his shouting till he got attended to – till she shook him by the arm, or thrust the mouthpiece of his pipe between his teeth. He was one of the few blind people who smoke. When he felt the hat being put on his head he stopped his noise at once. Then he rose, and they passed together through the gate.

He weighed heavily on her arm. During their slow, toilful walks she appeared to be dragging with her for a penance the burden of that infirm bulk. Usually they crossed the road at once (the cottages stood in the fields near the harbour, two hundred yards away from the end of the street), and for a long, long time they would remain in view, ascending imperceptibly the flight of wooden steps that led to the top of the sea-wall. It ran on from east to west, shutting out the Channel like a neglected railway embankment, on which no train had ever rolled within memory of man. Groups of sturdy fishermen would emerge upon the sky, walk along for a bit, and sink without haste. Their brown nets, like the cobwebs of gigantic spiders, lay on the shabby grass of the slope; and, looking up from the end of the street, the people of the town would recognise the two Carvils by the creeping slowness of their gait. Captain Hagberd, pottering aimlessly about his cottages, would raise his head to see how they got on in their promenade.

He advertised still in the Sunday papers for Harry Hagberd. These sheets were read in foreign parts to the end of the world, he informed Bessie. At the same time he seemed to think that his son was in England – so near to Colebrook that he would of course turn up 'to-morrow.' Bessie, without committing herself to that opinion in so many words, argued that in that case the expense of advertising was unnecessary; Captain Hagberd had better spend that weekly half-crown on himself. She declared she did not know what he lived on. Her argumentation would puzzle him and cast him down for a time. 'They all do it,' he pointed out. There was a whole column devoted to appeals after missing relatives. He would bring the newspaper to show her. He and his wife had advertised for years; only she was an impatient woman. The news from Colebrook had arrived the very day after her funeral; if she had not been so impatient she might have been here now, with no more than one day more to wait. 'You are not an impatient woman, my dear.'

'I've no patience with you sometimes,' she would say.

If he still advertised for his son he did not offer rewards for information any more; for, with the muddled lucidity of a mental derangement, he had reasoned himself into a conviction as clear as daylight that he had already attained all that could be expected in that way. What more could he want? Colebrook was the place, and there was no need to ask for more. Miss Carvil praised him for his good sense, and he was soothed by the part she took in his hope, which had become his delusion; in that idea which blinded his mind to truth and probability, just as the other old man in the other cottage had been made blind, by another disease, to the light and beauty of the world.

But anything he could interpret as a doubt – any coldness of assent, or even a simple inattention to the development of his projects of a home with his returned son and his son's wife – would irritate him into flings and jerks and wicked side-glances. He would dash his spade into the ground and walk to and fro before it. Miss Bessie called it his tantrums. She shook her finger at him. Then, when she came out again, after he had parted with her in anger, he would watch out of the corner of his eyes for the least sign of encouragement to approach the iron railings and resume his fatherly and patronising relations.

For all their intimacy, which had lasted some years now, they had never talked without a fence or a railing between them. He described to her all the splendours accumulated for the setting-up of their housekeeping, but had never invited her to an inspection. No human eye was to behold them till Harry had his first look.

In fact, nobody had ever been inside his cottage; he did his own housework, and he guarded his son's privilege so jealously that the small objects of domestic use he bought sometimes in the town were smuggled rapidly across the front garden under his canvas coat. Then, coming out, he would remark apologetically, 'It was only a small kettle, my dear.'

And, if not too tired with her drudgery, or worried beyond endurance by her father, she would laugh at him with a blush, and say: 'That's all right, Captain Hagberd; I am not impatient.'

'Well, my dear, you haven't long to wait now,' he would answer with a sudden bashfulness, and looking uneasily, as though he had suspected that there was something wrong somewhere.

Every Monday she paid him his rent over the railings. He clutched the shillings greedily. He grudged every penny he had to spend on his maintenance, and when he left her to make his purchases his bearing changed as soon as he got into the street. Away from the sanction of her pity, he felt himself exposed without defence. He brushed the walls with his shoulder. He mistrusted the queerness of the people; yet, by then, even the town children had left off calling after him, and the tradesmen served him without a word. The slightest allusion to his clothing had the power to puzzle and frighten especially, as if it were something utterly unwarranted and incomprehensible.

In the autumn, the driving rain drummed on his sail-cloth suit saturated almost to the stiffness of sheet-iron, with its surface flowing with water. When the weather was too bad, he retreated under the tiny porch, and, standing close against the door, looked at his spade left planted in the middle of the yard. The ground was so much dug up all over, that as the season advanced it turned to a quagmire. When it froze hard, he was disconsolate. What would Harry say? And as he could not have so much of Bessie's company at that time of the year, the roars of old Carvil, that came muffled through the closed windows, calling her indoors, exasperated him greatly.

'Why don't that extravagant fellow get you a servant?' he asked impatiently one mild afternoon. She had thrown something over her head to run out for a while.

'I don't know,' said the pale Bessie, wearily, staring away with her heavy-lidded, grey, and unexpectant glance. There were always smudgy shadows under her eyes, and she did not seem able to see any change or any end to her life.

'You wait till you get married, my dear,' said her only friend, drawing closer to the fence. 'Harry will get you one.'

His hopeful craze seemed to mock her own want of hope with so bitter an aptness that in her nervous irritation she could have screamed at him outright. But she only said in self-mockery, and speaking to him as though he had been sane, 'Why, Captain Hagberd, your son may not even want to look at me.'

He flung his head back and laughed his throaty affected cackle of anger.

'What! That boy? Not want to look at the only sensible girl for miles around? What do you think I am here for, my dear – my dear – my dear? . . . What? You wait. You just wait. You'll see to-morrow. I'll soon –'

'Bessie! Bessie! Bessie!' howled old Carvil inside. 'Bessie! – my pipe!' That fat blind man had given himself up to a very lust of laziness. He would not lift his hand to reach for the things she took care to leave at his very elbow. He would not move a limb; he would not rise from his chair; he would not put one foot before another, in that parlour (where he knew his way as well as if he had his sight), without calling her to his side and hanging all his atrocious weight on her shoulder. He would not eat one single mouthful of food without her close attendance. He had made himself helpless beyond his affliction, to enslave her better. She stood still for a moment, setting her teeth in the dusk, then turned and walked slowly indoors.

Captain Hagberd went back to his spade. The shouting in Carvil's cottage stopped, and after a while the window of the parlour downstairs was lit up. A man coming from the end of the street with a firm leisurely step passed on, but seemed to have caught sight of Captain Hagberd, because he turned back a pace or two. A cold white light lingered in the western sky. The man leaned over the gate in an interested manner.

'You must be Captain Hagberd,' he said, with easy assurance.

The old man spun round, pulling out his spade, startled by the strange voice.

'Yes, I am,' he answered nervously.

The other, smiling straight at him, uttered very

slowly: 'You've been advertising for your son, I believe?'

'My son Harry,' mumbled Captain Hagberd, off his guard for once. 'He's coming home to-morrow.'

'The devil he is!' The stranger marvelled greatly, and then went on, with only a slight change of tone: 'You've grown a beard like Father Christmas himself.'

Captain Hagberd drew a little nearer, and leaned forward over his spade. 'Go your way,' he said, resentfully and timidly at the same time, because he was always afraid of being laughed at. Every mental state, even madness, has its equilibrium based upon self-esteem. Its disturbance causes unhappiness; and Captain Hagberd lived amongst a scheme of settled notions which it pained him to feel disturbed by people's grins. Yes, people's grins were awful. They hinted at something wrong: but what? He could not tell; and that stranger was obviously grinning – had come on purpose to grin. It was bad enough on the streets, but he had never before been outraged like this.

The stranger, unaware how near he was of having his head laid open with a spade, said seriously: 'I am not trespassing where I stand, am I? I fancy there's something wrong about your news. Suppose you let me come in.'

'*You* come in!' murmured old Hagberd, with inexpressible horror.

'I could give you some real information about your son – the very latest tip, if you care to hear.'

'No,' shouted Hagberd. He began to pace wildly to and fro, he shouldered his spade, he gesticulated with his other arm. 'Here's a fellow – a grinning fellow, who says there's something wrong. I've got more information than you're aware of. I've all the information I want. I've had it for years – for years – for years – enough to last me till to-morrow. Let you come in, indeed! What would Harry say?'

Bessie Carvil's figure appeared in black silhouette on the parlour window; then, with the sound of an opening door, flitted out before the other cottage, all black, but with something white over her head. These two voices beginning to talk suddenly outside (she had heard them indoors) had given her such an emotion that she could not utter a sound.

Captain Hagberd seemed to be trying to find his way out of a cage. His feet squelched in the puddles left by his industry. He stumbled in the holes of the ruined grass-plot. He ran blindly against the fence.

'Here, steady a bit!' said the man at the gate, gravely stretching his arm over and catching him by the sleeve. 'Somebody's been trying to get at you. Hallo! what's this rig you've got on? Storm canvas, by George!' He had a big laugh. 'Well, you *are* a character!'

Captain Hagberd jerked himself free, and began to back away shrinkingly. 'For the present,' he muttered, in a crestfallen tone.

'What's the matter with him?' The stranger addressed Bessie with the utmost familiarity, in a deliberate, explanatory tone. 'I didn't want to startle the old man.' He lowered his voice as though he had known her for years. 'I dropped into a barber's on my way, to get a twopenny shave, and they told me there he was something of a character. The old man has been a character all his life.'

Captain Hagberd, daunted by the allusion to his clothing, had retreated inside, taking his spade with him; and the two at the gate, startled by the unexpected slamming of the door, heard the bolts being shot, the snapping of the lock, and the echo of an affected gurgling laugh within.

'I didn't want to upset him,' the man said, after a short silence. 'What's the meaning of all this? He isn't quite crazy.'

'He has been worrying a long time about his lost son,' said Bessie, in a low apologetic tone.

'Well, I am his son.'

'Harry!' she cried – and was profoundly silent.

'Know my name? Friends with the old man, eh?'

'He's our landlord,' Bessie faltered out, catching hold of the iron railing.

'Owns both them rabbit-hutches, does he?' commented young Hagberd, scornfully. 'Just the thing he would be proud of. Can you tell me who's that chap coming to-morrow? You must know something of it. I tell you, it's a swindle on the old man – nothing else.'

She did not answer, helpless before an insurmountable difficulty, appalled before the necessity, the impossibility and the dread of an explanation in which she and madness seemed involved together.

'Oh – I am so sorry,' she murmured.

'What's the matter?' he said, with serenity. 'You

needn't be afraid of upsetting me. It's the other fellow that'll be upset when he least expects it. I don't care a hang; but there will be some fun when he shows his mug to-morrow. I don't care *that* for the old man's pieces, but right is right. You shall see me put a head on that coon – whoever he is!'

He had come nearer, and towered above her on the other side of the railings. He glanced at her hands. He fancied she was trembling, and it occurred to him that she had her part perhaps in that little game that was to be sprung on his old man to-morrow. He had come just in time to spoil their sport. He was entertained by the idea – scornful of the baffled plot. But all his life he had been full of indulgence for all sorts of women's tricks. She really was trembling very much; her wrap had slipped off her head. 'Poor devil!' he thought. 'Never mind about that chap. I daresay he'll change his mind before to-morrow. But what about me? I can't loaf about the gate till the morning.'

She burst out: 'It is *you* – you yourself that he's waiting for. It is *you* who come to-morrow.'

He murmured 'Oh! It's me!' blankly, and they seemed to become breathless together. Apparently he was pondering over what he had heard; then, without irritation, but evidently perplexed, he said: 'I don't understand. I hadn't written or anything. It's my chum who saw the paper and told me – this very morning . . . Eh? what?'

He bent his ear; she whispered rapidly, and he listened for a while, muttering the words 'yes' and 'I see' at times. Then, 'But why won't to-day do?' he queried at last.

'You didn't understand me!' she exclaimed, impatiently. The clear streak of light under the clouds died out in the west. Again he stooped slightly to hear better; and the deep night buried everything of the whispering woman and the attentive man, except the familiar contiguity of their faces, with its air of secrecy and caress.

He squared his shoulders; the broad-brimmed shadow of a hat sat cavalierly on his head. 'Awkward this, eh?' he appealed to her. 'To-morrow? Well, well! Never heard tell of anything like this. It's all to-morrow, then, without any sort of to-day, as far as I can see.'

She remained still and mute.

'And you have been encouraging this funny notion,' he said.

'I never contradicted him.'

'Why didn't you?'

'What for should I?' she defended herself. 'It would only have made him miserable. He would have gone out of his mind.'

'His mind!' he muttered, and heard a short nervous laugh from her.

'Where was the harm? Was I to quarrel with the poor old man? It was easier to half believe it myself.'

'Aye, aye,' he meditated, intelligently. 'I suppose the old chap got around you somehow with his soft talk. You are good-hearted.'

Her hands moved up in the dark nervously. 'And it might have been true. It was true. It has come. Here it is. This is the to-morrow we have been waiting for.'

She drew a breath, and he said, good-humouredly: 'Aye, with the door shut. I wouldn't care if . . . And you think he could be brought round to recognise me . . . Eh? What? . . . You could do it? In a week you say? H'm, I daresay you could – but do you think I could hold out a week in this dead-alive place? Not me! I want either hard work, or an all-fired racket, or more space than there is in the whole of England. I have been in this place, though, once before, and for more than a week. The old man was advertising for me then, and a chum I had with me had a notion of getting a couple of quid out of him by writing a lot of silly nonsense in a letter. That lark did not come off, though. We had to clear out – and none too soon. But this time I've a chum waiting for me in London, and besides . . .'

Bessie Carvil was breathing quickly.

'What if I tried a knock at the door?' he suggested.

'Try,' she said.

Captain Hagberd's gate squeaked, and the shadow of the son moved on, then stopped with another deep laugh in the throat, like the father's, only soft and gentle, thrilling to the woman's heart, awakening to her ears.

'He isn't frisky – is he? I would be afraid to lay hold of him. The chaps are always telling me I don't know my own strength.'

'He's the most harmless creature that ever lived,' she interrupted.

'You wouldn't say so if you had seen him chasing me upstairs with a hard leather strap,' he said. 'I haven't forgotten it in sixteen years.'

She got warm from head to foot under another soft, subdued laugh. At the rat-tat-tat of the knocker her heart flew into her mouth.

'Hey, dad! Let me in. I am Harry, I am. Straight! Come back home a day too soon.'

One of the windows upstairs ran up.

'A grinning information fellow,' said the voice of old Hagberd, up in the darkness. 'Don't you have anything to do with him. It will spoil everything.'

She heard Harry Hagberd say, 'Hallo, dad,' then a clanging clatter. The window rumbled down, and he stood before her again.

'It's just like old times. Nearly walloped the life out of me to stop me going away, and now I come back he throws a confounded shovel at my head to keep me out. It grazed my shoulder.'

She shuddered.

'I wouldn't care,' he began, 'only I spent my last shillings on the railway fare and my last twopence on a shave – out of respect for the old man.'

'Are you really Harry Hagberd?' she asked swiftly. 'Can you prove it?'

'Can I prove it? Can any one else prove it?' he said jovially. 'Prove with what? What do I want to prove?

There isn't a single corner in the world, barring England, perhaps, where you could not find some man, or more likely a woman, that would remember me for Harry Hagberd. I am more like Harry Hagberd than any man alive; and I can prove it to you in a minute, if you will let me step inside your gate.'

'Come in,' she said.

He entered then the front garden of the Carvils. His tall shadow strode with a swagger; she turned her back on the window and waited, watching the shape, of which the footfalls seemed the most material part. The light fell on a tilted hat; a powerful shoulder that seemed to cleave the darkness; on a leg stepping out. He swung about and stood still, facing the illuminated parlour window at her back, turning his head from side to side, laughing softly to himself.

'Just fancy, for a minute, the old man's beard stuck on to my chin. Hey? Now say. I was the very spit of him from a boy.'

'It's true,' she murmured to herself.

'And that's about as far as it goes. He was always one of your domestic characters. Why, I remember how he used to go about looking very sick for three days before he had to leave home on one of his trips to South Shields for coal. He had a standing charter from the gas-works. You would think he was off on a whaling cruise – three years and a tail. Ha, ha! Not a bit of it. Ten days on the outside. The *Skimmer of the Seas* was a smart craft. Fine name, wasn't it? Mother's uncle owned her . . .'

He interrupted himself, and in a lowered voice, 'Did he ever tell you what mother died of?' he asked.

'Yes,' said Miss Bessie, bitterly: 'from impatience.'

He made no sound for a while; then brusquely: 'They were so afraid I would turn out badly that they fairly drove me away. Mother nagged at me for being idle, and the old man said he would cut my soul out of my body rather than let me go to sea. Well, it looked as if he would do it too – so I went. It looks to me sometimes as if I had been born to them by a mistake – in that other hutch of a house.'

'Where ought you to have been born by rights?' Bessie Carvil interrupted him, defiantly.

'In the open, upon a beach, on a windy night,' he said, quick as lightning. Then he mused slowly. 'They were characters, both of them, by George; and the old man keeps it up well – don't he? A damned shovel on the – Hark! who's that making that row? "Bessie, Bessie." It's in your house.'

'It's for me,' she said with indifference.

He stepped aside, out of the streak of light. 'Your husband?' he inquired, with the tone of a man accustomed to unlawful trysts. 'Fine voice for a ship's deck in a thundering squall.'

'No; my father. I am not married.'

'You seem a fine girl, Miss Bessie, dear,' he said at once. She turned her face away.

'Oh, I say, what's up? Who's murdering him?'

'He wants his tea.' She faced him, still and tall, with averted head, with her hands hanging clasped before her.

'Hadn't you better go in?' he suggested, after watching for a while the nape of her neck, a patch of dazzling white skin and soft shadow above the sombre line of her shoulders. Her wrap had slipped down to her elbows. 'You'll have all the town coming out presently. I'll wait here a bit.'

Her wrap fell to the ground, and he stooped to pick it up; she had vanished. He threw it over his arm, and approaching the window squarely he saw a monstrous form of a fat man in an arm-chair, an unshaded lamp, the yawning of an enormous mouth in a big flat face encircled by a ragged halo of hair, Miss Bessie's head and bust. The shouting stopped; the blind ran down. He lost himself in thinking how awkward it was. Father mad; no getting into the house. No money to get back; a hungry chum in London who would begin to think he had been given the go-by. 'Damn!' he muttered. He could break the door in, certainly; but they would perhaps bundle him into chokey for that without asking questions – no great matter, only he was confoundedly afraid of being locked up, even in mistake. He turned cold at the thought. He stamped his feet on the sodden grass.

'What are you? A sailor?' said an agitated voice.

She had flitted out, a shadow herself, attracted by the reckless shadow waiting under the wall of her home.

'Anything. Enough of a sailor to be worth my salt before the mast. Came home that way this time.'

'Where do you come from?' she asked.

'Right away from a jolly good spree,' he said, 'by

the London train – see? Ough! I hate being shut up in a train. I don't mind a house so much.'

'Ah,' she said, 'that's lucky.'

'Because in a house you can at any time open the blamed door and walk away straight before you.'

'And never come back?'

'Not for sixteen years at least,' he laughed. 'To a rabbit-hutch, and get a confounded old shovel . . .'

'A ship is not so very big,' she taunted.

'No, but the sea is great.'

She dropped her head, and as if her ears had been opened to the voices of the world, she heard, beyond the rampart of sea-wall, the swell of yesterday's gale breaking on the beach with monotonous and solemn vibrations, as if all the earth had been a tolling bell.

'And then, why, a ship's a ship. You love her and leave her; and a voyage isn't a marriage.' He quoted the sailor's saying lightly.

'It is not a marriage,' she whispered.

'I never took a false name, and I've never yet told a lie to a woman. What lie? Why, *the* lie –. Take me or leave me, I say: and if you take me, then it is . . .' He hummed a snatch very low, leaning against the wall.

Oh, ho, ho Rio!
And fare thee well,
My bonnie young girl,
We're bound to Rio Grande.

'Capstan song,' he explained. Her teeth chattered.

'You are cold,' he said. 'Here's that affair of yours I picked up.' She felt his hands about her, wrapping her closely. 'Hold the ends together in front,' he commanded.

'What did you come here for?' she asked, repressing a shudder.

'Five quid,' he answered, promptly. 'We let our spree go on a little too long and got hard up.'

'You've been drinking?' she said.

'Blind three days; on purpose. I am not given that way – don't you think. There's nothing and nobody that can get over me unless I like. I can be as steady as a rock. My chum sees the paper this morning, and says he to me: "Go on, Harry: loving parent. That's five quid sure." So we scraped all our pockets for the fare. Devil of a lark!'

'You have a hard heart, I am afraid,' she sighed.

'What for? For running away? Why! he wanted to

make a lawyer's clerk of me – just to please himself. Master in his own house; and my poor mother egged him on – for my good, I suppose. Well, then – so long; and I went. No, I tell you: the day I cleared out, I was all black and blue from his great fondness for me. Ah! he was always a bit of a character. Look at that shovel now. Off his chump? Not much. That's just exactly like my dad. He wants me here just to have somebody to order about. However, we two were hard up; and what's five quid to him – once in sixteen hard years?'

'Oh, but I am sorry for you. Did you never want to come back home?'

'Be a lawyer's clerk and rot here – in some such place as this?' he cried in contempt. 'What! if the old man set me up in a home to-day, I would kick it down about my ears – or else die there before the third day was out.'

'And where else is it that you hope to die?'

'In the bush somewhere; in the sea; on a blamed mountaintop for choice. At home? Yes! the world's my home; but I expect I'll die in a hospital some day. What of that? Any place is good enough, as long as I've lived; and I've been everything you can think of almost but a tailor or a soldier. I've been a boundary rider; I've sheared sheep; and humped my swag; and harpooned a whale. I've rigged ships, and prospected for gold, and skinned dead bullocks – and turned my back on more money than the old man would have scraped in his whole life. Ha, ha!'

He overwhelmed her. She pulled herself together and managed to utter, 'Time to rest now.'

He straightened himself up, away from the wall, and in a severe voice said, 'Time to go.'

But he did not move. He leaned back again, and hummed thoughtfully a bar or two of an outlandish tune.

She felt as if she were about to cry. 'That's another of your cruel songs,' she said.

'Learned it in Mexico – in Sonora.' He talked easily. 'It is the song of the Gambusinos. You don't know? The song of restless men. Nothing could hold them in one place – not even a woman. You used to meet one of them now and again, in the old days, on the edge of the gold country, away north there beyond the Rio Gila. I've seen it. A prospecting engineer in Mazatlan took me along with him to help look after the waggons. A sailor's a handy chap to have about you anyhow. It's all a desert: cracks in the earth that you can't see the bottom of; and mountains – sheer rocks standing up high like walls and church spires, only a hundred times bigger. The valleys are full of boulders and black stones. There's not a blade of grass to see; and the sun sets more red over that country than I have seen it anywhere – blood-red and angry. It *is* fine.'

'You do not want to go back there again?' she stammered out.

He laughed a little. 'No. That's the blamed gold country. It gave me the shivers sometimes to look at it – and we were a big lot of men together, mind; but these Gambusinos wandered alone. They knew that country before anybody had ever heard of it. They had a sort of gift for prospecting, and the fever of it was on them too; and they did not seem to want the gold very much. They would find some rich spot, and then turn their backs on it; pick up perhaps a little – enough for a spree – and then be off again, looking for more. They never stopped long where there were houses; they had no wife, no chick, no home, never a chum. You couldn't be friends with a Gambusino; they were too restless – here to-day, and gone, God

knows where, to-morrow. They told no one of their
finds, and there has never been a Gambusino well
off. It was not for the gold they cared; it was the
wandering about looking for it in the stony country
that got into them and wouldn't let them rest; so that
no woman yet born could hold a Gambusino for more
than a week. That's what the song says. It's all about
a pretty girl that tried hard to keep hold of a Gambusino lover, so that he should bring her lots of gold.
No fear! Off he went, and she never saw him again.'

'What became of her?' she breathed out.

'The song don't tell. Cried a bit, I daresay. They
were the fellows: kiss and go. But it's the looking for
a thing – a something . . . Sometimes I think I am a
sort of Gambusino myself.'

'No woman can hold you, then,' she began in a bra-
zen voice, which quavered suddenly before the end.

'No longer than a week,' he joked, playing upon
her very heartstrings with the gay, tender note of his
laugh, 'and yet I am fond of them all. Anything for
a woman of the right sort. The scrapes they got me
into, and the scrapes they got me out of! I love them
at first sight. I've fallen in love with you already,
Miss – Bessie's your name – eh?'

She backed away a little, and with a trembling laugh: 'You haven't seen my face yet.'

He bent forward gallantly. 'A little pale: it suits some. But you are a fine figure of a girl, Miss Bessie.'

She was all in a flutter. Nobody had ever said so much to her before.

His tone changed. 'I am getting middling hungry, though. Had no breakfast to-day. Couldn't you scare up some bread from that tea for me, or –'

She was gone already. He had been on the point of asking her to let him come inside. No matter. Anywhere would do. Devil of a fix! What would his chum think?

'I didn't ask you as a beggar,' he said, jestingly, taking a piece of bread-and-butter from the plate she held before him. 'I asked as a friend. My dad is rich, you know.'

'He starves himself for your sake.'

'And I have starved for his whim,' he said, taking up another piece.

'All he has in the world is for you,' she pleaded.

'Yes, if I come here to sit on it like a dam' toad in

a hole. Thank you; and what about the shovel, eh? He always had a queer way of showing his love.'

'I could bring him round in a week,' she suggested timidly.

He was too hungry to answer her; and, holding the plate submissively to his hand, she began to whisper up to him in a quick, panting voice. He listened, amazed, eating slower and slower, till at last his jaws stopped altogether. 'That's his game, is it?' he said, in a rising tone of scathing contempt. An ungovernable movement of his arm sent the plate flying out of her fingers. He shot out a violent curse.

She shrank from him, putting her hand against the wall.

'No!' he raged. 'He expects! Expects *me* – for his rotten money! . . . Who wants his home? Mad – not he! Don't you think? He wants his own way. He wanted to turn me into a miserable lawyer's clerk, and now he wants to make of me a blamed tame rabbit in a cage. Of me! Of me!' His subdued angry laugh frightened her now.

'The whole world ain't a bit too big for me to spread my elbows in, I can tell you – what's your name – Bessie – let alone a dam' parlour in a hutch. Marry! He wants me to marry and settle! And as likely as not he has looked out the girl too – dash my soul! And do you know the Judy, may I ask?'

She shook all over with noiseless dry sobs; but he was fuming and fretting too much to notice her distress. He bit his thumb with rage at the mere idea. A window rattled up.

'A grinning information fellow,' pronounced old Hagberd dogmatically, in measured tones. And the sound of his voice seemed to Bessie to make the night itself mad – to pour insanity and disaster on the earth. 'Now I know what's wrong with the people here, my dear. Why, of course! With this mad chap going about. Don't you have anything to do with him, Bessie. Bessie, I say!'

They stood as if dumb. The old man fidgeted and mumbled to himself at the window. Suddenly he cried, piercingly: 'Bessie – I see you. I'll tell Harry.'

She made a movement as if to run away, but stopped and raised her hands to her temples. Young Hagberd, shadowy and big, stirred no more than a man of bronze. Over their heads the crazy night whimpered and scolded in an old man's voice.

'Send him away, my dear. He's only a vagabond. What you want is a good home of your own. That chap has no home – he's not like Harry. He can't be Harry. Harry is coming to-morrow. Do you hear? One day more,' he babbled more excitedly. 'Never you fear – Harry shall marry you.'

His voice rose very shrill and mad against the regular deep soughing of the swell coiling heavily about the outer face of the sea-wall.

'He will have to. I shall make him, or if not' – he swore a great oath – 'I'll cut him off with a shilling to-morrow, and leave everything to you. I shall. To you. Let him starve.'

The window rattled down.

Harry drew a deep breath, and took one step towards Bessie. 'So it's you – the girl,' he said, in a lowered voice. She had not moved, and she remained half turned away from him, pressing her head in the palms of her hands. 'My world!' he continued, with an invisible half-smile on his lips. 'I have a great mind to stop . . .'

Her elbows were trembling violently.

'For a week,' he finished without a pause.

She clapped her hands to her face.

He came up quite close, and took hold of her wrists gently. She felt his breath on her ear.

'It's a scrape I am in – this, and it is you that must see me through.' He was trying to uncover her face. She resisted. He let her go then, and stepping back a little, 'Have you got any money?' he asked. 'I must be off now.'

She nodded quickly her shamefaced head, and he waited, looking away from her, while, trembling all over and bowing her neck, she tried to find the pocket of her dress.

'Here it is!' she whispered. 'Oh, go away! Go away for God's sake! If I had more – more – I would give it all to forget – to make you forget.'

He extended his hand. 'No fear! I haven't forgotten a single one of you in the world. Some gave me more than money – but I am a beggar now – and you women always had to get me out of my scrapes.'

He swaggered up to the parlour window, and in the dim light filtering through the blind, looked at the coin lying in his palm. It was a half-sovereign. He slipped it into his pocket. She stood a little on one side, with her head drooping, as if wounded; with her arms hanging passive by her side, as if dead.

'You can't buy me in,' he said, 'and you can't buy yourself out.'

He set his hat firmly with a little tap, and next moment she felt herself lifted up in the powerful embrace of his arms. Her feet lost the ground; her head hung back; he showered kisses on her face with a silent and overmastering ardour, as if in haste to get at her very soul. He kissed her pale cheeks, her hard forehead, her heavy eyelids, her faded lips; and the measured blows and sighs of the rising tide accompanied the enfolding power of his arms, the overwhelming might of his caresses. It was as if the sea, breaking down the wall protecting all the homes of the town, had sent a wave over her head. It passed on; she staggered backwards, with her shoulders against the wall, exhausted, as if she had been stranded there after a storm and a shipwreck.

She opened her eyes after a while; and, listening to the firm, leisurely footsteps going away with their conquest, began to gather her skirts, staring all the time before her. Suddenly she darted through the open gate into the dark and deserted street.

'Stop!' she shouted. 'Don't go!'

And listening with an attentive poise of the head,

she could not tell whether it was the beat of the swell or his fateful tread that seemed to fall cruelly upon her heart. Presently every sound grew fainter, as though she were slowly turning into stone. A fear of this awful silence came to her – worse than the fear of death. She called upon her ebbing strength for the final appeal:

'Harry!'

Not even the dying echo of a footstep. Nothing. The thundering of the surf, the voice of the restless sea itself, seemed stopped. There was not a sound – no whisper of life, as though she were alone and lost in that stony country of which she had heard, where madmen go looking for gold and spurn the find.

Captain Hagberd, inside his dark house, had kept on the alert. A window ran up; and in the silence of the stony country a voice spoke above her head, high up in the black air – the voice of madness, lies and despair – the voice of inextinguishable hope. 'Is he gone yet – that information fellow? Do you hear him about, my dear?'

She burst into tears. 'No! no! no! I don't hear him any more,' she sobbed.

He began to chuckle up there triumphantly. 'You

frightened him away. Good girl. Now we shall be all right. Don't you be impatient, my dear. One day more.'

In the other house old Carvil, wallowing regally in his arm-chair, with a globe-lamp burning by his side on the table, yelled for her, in a fiendish voice: 'Bessie! Bessie! You, Bessie!'

She heard him at last, and, as if overcome by fate, began to totter silently back towards her stuffy little inferno of a cottage. It had no lofty portal, no terrific inscription of forfeited hopes – she did not understand wherein she had sinned.

Captain Hagberd had gradually worked himself into a state of noisy happiness up there.

'Go in! Keep quiet!' she turned upon him tearfully, from the doorstep below.

He rebelled against her authority in his great joy at having got rid at last of that 'something wrong.' It was as if all the hopeful madness of the world had broken out to bring terror upon her heart, with the voice of that old man shouting of his trust in an everlasting to-morrow.